SENSUAL SEX TALES

EXPLICIT DIRTY EROTICA SHORT STORIES

FAE DEROSE

plicit Press

CHAPTER 1

IN THE SHADOWS

THE GYM WAS empty save one lone soldier. Twenty-year-old Ranie was on her second set of reps, her fair skin glistening with sweat. Her short black waves hung in wet strands; her cheeks were red with exertion. All of the other agents, including Ranie's sister, had turned in hours before, but Ranie kept pushing. Rumor had it that the higher-ups were looking for a new team dynamic, including new first and second positions. Ranie fully intended to be on that team.

Muscles burning, heart racing, Ranie set down the weights and let out a rush of air. She started for the locker room, letting her body cool down on the way.

The faintest squeak of a shoe and a flutter of a shadow made Ranie's eyes flick to one side, but her steps didn't falter. The whisper of socks turned to the gentle pad of bare feet. Ranie let a small smile play over her lips and pulled off her black sports bra, exposing her firm breasts, caramel-colored nipples hardened into pebbles. She tossed the garment into a nearby basket as she passed, not stopping until she reached the showers.

She felt his eyes on her as she shimmied out of her pants and kicked them back into the room. She turned on the nearest shower and stepped under the warm spray. She closed her gray eyes, letting the water rinse away the evidence of her workout. After a moment, she worked the shampoo into a lather and then filled a washcloth with soap.

It would be nice, she thought, to have something scented every once in a while. Just once, she'd like to bathe in something that made her smell like vanilla or strawberries or something like that. She sighed, purposefully turning into the spray to rinse away the last of the soap, giving him the perfect opportunity to strike.

Muscled arms slid around her waist, and pulled her back against a body that was as familiar to her as her own. His blond hair was short, so the water would've already soaked in, turning it almost brown. His green eyes would be dark with lust, nearly black. Her hands had mapped the plains of his sculpted torso so often that she knew every dip and ridge. She knew the rough edge of the scar that ran almost the full length of his right arm. The scar across his broad shoulders was where the glass from a broken window had sliced into his flesh two years before he'd come to the Shadow Project. Then there was the burn at the small of his back, just above the swell of his ass. She knew it all.

And then there was the hardest part of him, hot and heavy against her hip. She loved the feel of him in her hand, in her mouth, the taste of him on her tongue. After eighteen months, she still wasn't tired of him. More than anything, she wanted an outside assignment with him so they'd be able to have more than just a quick fuck they could pass off as stress relief or recreation. Anything more strictly forbidden and the pair was well aware of the consequences if anyone at the Project had known how they truly felt.

Forcible separation would be the best result, elimination the most likely, especially if the Project wanted to make an example of them.

Ranie pushed the thought from her mind to focus on the moment at hand. "Zak," his name was a breath, a sigh.

"I love watching you train," Zak's voice ran over her skin like molten lava, sending shivers down her spine and making her wet in a way that had nothing to do with the shower. Ranie loved when he spoke in that tone, a low, husky sound that was only for her. He wasn't a very verbal man, but even a few choice words could make her squirm, make her burn.

"I love it when you watch me," Ranie countered. His eyes on her always made her work harder, move faster.

Zak moved her forward until she was pressed against the wall, the tiles cool against her feverish skin, smooth and slick against her hard nipples. His hands dropped from her waist, one sliding around to her hip, the other falling to the juncture between her legs. His fingers skimmed over the coarse curls to delve between her folds. Ranie's head fell back against his chest as he stroked expertly over her clit before moving lower to slip a finger into her core.

"Fuck," she whispered. Zak knew how to play her body like a fine instrument and she writhed in his arms, parting her legs to give him better access.

"That's the general idea," he chuckled, a rare sound that nearly made Ranie cum right there.

The whimper that came at the withdrawal of his finger turned into a groan of satisfaction as he sank his full length into her aching pussy. It had been far too long since he'd been inside her and she came instantly. Zak gave her no respite, no time to adjust to the sudden feeling of fullness. Even as her body shook around him, he began to thrust, every stroke rubbing right over that delicious spot inside her, sending another wave of pleasure through her.

Water cascaded over them both, each drop adding to the sensations filling her body until she thought she could bear no more. Zak's mouth dropped to the spot where her neck met her shoulder and he worked at the skin, sucking it into his mouth, marking her so that the other recruits would know that she was taken. Not that there had ever been any doubt. From the moment he'd touched her, Zak had been the only one she'd ever wanted. She knew what was coming next and her body tensed in anticipation, wanting it, wanting to lose herself again.

Zak shoved himself hard and deep, biting down on the flesh in his mouth as he came. Ranie shattered around him, crying out his name as she climaxed. They sank together to the floor, his arms wrapped around her, his mouth whispering in her ear.

"Only you."

Ranie nodded in agreement, still dragging in shuddering gasps of air as her muscles trembled beneath her skin. They only had a few minutes they could pass off as recovery before the ever-watching Shadow Project would start getting suspicious. All too soon, Zak stood, letting the water wash away the evidence of their encounter.

"Good fuck," he grinned, the expression in his eyes telling her that he wished he could say something far different.

"You too," Ranie got to her feet, legs still a bit shaky. As she watched him go, in that moment, she knew that she would do anything to get them both on the next team together. Anything to give them the opportunity to be with each other without having to hide how they felt about each other. For the first time since joining the Project, she wondered if it was truly worth the price.

CHAPTER 2

THE GREATEST GIFT

"SO, Lonan, Elly tells me that you're an artist," Major Walter Summers glowered across the room at his daughter's twenty-five-year-old boyfriend. Lonan Wilcox tried not to squirm under the steel gaze. Mr. Summers may have had the same cornflower blue eyes as his twenty-three-year-old daughter, but they had none of her warmth.

"Yes, sir," Lonan ran his hand through his ebony hair. "I do freelance work mostly. Graphic novels, logos, and such."

"He's had two pieces accepted by a local gallery for a show after the first of the year," Elly appeared from the kitchen, followed by her mother. Both were tall and slender with rich chestnut brown hair, though Elly had cut hers short just a few months before.

"That's wonderful," Mrs. Summers smiled at Lonan and he felt some of his tension ease. "Maybe Walter and I will head into the city to see it."

"We will?" The major glared at his wife who simply raised her eyebrow and handed him a mug of coffee.

"That would be lovely," Elly sat next to Lonan and reached for his hand. He hesitated, bottle-green eyes flicking towards her father. "We'd really love for you to see our place."

The expression on the major's face darkened and Elly tightened her grip on Lonan's hand as if she'd known he'd planned to let go. They'd been dating for a little over a year and had just moved in together two months ago. Lonan had wanted to wait until he met her parents, but Elly's lease had expired in October and it had just made sense. Now, he was starting to wonder if they'd made the right choice. Her parents had both known about him and about the move before they'd arrived, but Lonan could feel the disapproval radiating off of Major Summers from the moment they'd stepped through the door.

"The house looks amazing, Mrs. Summers," Lonan gestured to the tasteful Christmas decorations. "It reminds me of Christmas when I was a kid."

"Thank you, Lonan," Mrs. Summers sat in the chair next to her husband.

"Don't your parents decorate anymore?" The major crossed his arms and glared.

Elly made a sound next to him but Lonan squeezed her hand. He wasn't about to make things worse. "My parents died when I was fifteen. I lived with a distant cousin until I turned eighteen and moved out on my own."

"Elly," Mrs. Summers' voice was soft. "Why don't you take Lonan on a tour of the house? I'd like a word alone with your father before we open gifts."

Without a word, Lonan followed Elly from the living room. It wasn't until she led him up the stairs and down the hall that she spoke. "This is my room." She pulled him after her through a door and into a bedroom.

Lonan barely had enough time to register the evidence of Elly as a teenager before she was kissing him, dragging him back toward her bed. He knew he should protest, should pull away as her hands worked open his pants, but his brain couldn't seem to tell his body what to do. Then her hand was in his boxers, fingers closing around his cock and he couldn't think about anything but the woman in his arms. His tongue explored her mouth, relearning every curve and dip as the taste of her mother's cocoa exploded across his taste buds. As they tumbled onto her bed, his hands made their way under her sweater, pushing her bra up above her small breasts. His palms skimmed over her nipples and they hardened, as he'd known they would. He knew her body better than his own, could see in his mind's eye the delicate pink of the flesh he was rolling between his fingers.

"Lonan," Elly gasped as she tore their mouths apart. She shoved him onto his back and yanked his pants down around his hips.

He was fully erect now, all eight inches bobbing in the air, swollen with need. He blinked at her as she reached beneath her ankle-length skirt, the haze of pleasure that had been clouding her mind slowly clearing. He was hard enough that it wouldn't be pleasant if he stopped, but there was no way she was going to do what he thought.

Then came the unmistakable sound of pantyhose ripping and his cock twitched. "Elly," the word was a question and a plea all in one.

She straddled his lap, knees on either side of his waist. The black velvet of her skirt covered all but a creamy strip of the thigh where the slit rode up the side. Her hand was hidden under the material and he jumped when her fingers wrapped around him. A moment later, he felt the wet heat of her pussy against his tip, the faint touch of satin on one side telling him that she'd pulled aside the crotch of her panties.

"I don't care what he says," Elly placed both of her hands on his chest and let the first-inch slide inside. "Lonan Wilcox, you are an amazing man." Another inch and she gasped. "And I love you."

Lonan nearly cried out as she dropped the rest of the way, instantly encasing his cock in the heated silk of her pussy. Only the knowledge that her parents were downstairs held him in check. He bit down on his lip, back arching with the struggle to keep quiet. As she began to ride him, he shoved his hand into his mouth, muffling his sounds of pleasure.

"You feel so good inside me," Elly's legs flexed beneath her skirt as she rose up, just the tip remaining inside. She slowly lowered herself back down, each inch agonizing ecstasy. "The perfect fit."

"Elly, Lonan," Mrs. Summer's voice broke through their personal bubble. "We're ready to open

gifts."

"Just a minute, Mom," Elly called back, voice shockingly normal. Her eyes were darkened to the shade of a summer afternoon sky as she locked eyes with Lonan. Her voice dropped. "Let's finish this."

Lonan's entire body stiffened as Elly's pussy squeezed tight around him. His teeth clamped down on the side of his hand as she began to ride faster, hips alternating back and forth movements with up and down ones, each one sending a new wave of pleasure through him until he felt the familiar tightening in his balls, the pressure reaching the point where he knew he was going to explode. "Cum inside me, baby," Elly whispered. "I want to feel your cum inside me the rest of the

night. Every time my father says something to make you feel like we shouldn't be together, I want you to remember that I have you deep in my pussy."

His climax crashed into him, cock pulsing as it emptied inside her and he heard her call his name, felt her body spasming around him as she followed him over the edge. She fell forward, resting against his chest for a moment as their breathing slowed, their heartbeats returning to normal.

"Thank you for the lovely evening, Mrs. Summers," Lonan extended a hand.

"You're very welcome, Lonan," Mrs. Summers ignored his hand and drew him into her arms. "And ignore my husband." She whispered in his ear. "You and Elly are perfect for each other."

"I think so too," he whispered back.

As he stepped back, Elly handed him his coat and then glanced behind her at her dad. The major scowled.

"Dad."

. . .

Lonan could hear the warning in her tone.

"All right," the major growled. He took a step forward and held out a hand. "You seem like a good guy, Lonan. Treat my little girl right and you'll have no quarrel with me."

"Yes, sir, I will," Lonan shook Mr. Summers's hand, working to conceal his surprise.

As he and Elly walked down the sidewalk to their car, he asked, "How did you do that?"

Elly leaned her head on his shoulder. "I just told my dad that if he was going to be rude to the man I loved, maybe we shouldn't come around much." She placed a kiss on his cheek before reaching for the passenger side door. "Now, let's hurry home. I need a shower." She winked. "I'm a bit sticky."

CHAPTER 3

HER CHRISTMAS GIFT – AN EROTIC TALE

SHE PALMED HER NIPPLES, rotating her hands, gently caressing her breasts. She was very much overstimulated from both encounters and longed for her own release. She ran her hands down her sides and hips, wincing at the places her late husband Tony had held her. Looking down, she remembered seeing bruises in the exact shape of his fingertips, half-moon marks where his nails had broken the skin. She longed to feel him, touch him again. Mary knew with Tony dead, it would be a very lonely Christmas.

Her husband Tony had recently passed away in a terrible car crash, just a few months ago.

Mary sighed. Her relationship with Tony hadn't been the best. She'd been arguing with him the morning of the crash, begging him to work less.

She turned back to the water, letting the stream wash over her face.

Christmas was a time for family and friends, but here she was, lonelier than ever. Mary wished she'd pushed the idea of starting a family with her husband before he died.

Her hands were between her legs now and had found

her clitoris. She was very aroused and frustrated as well. Her clit was exquisitely sensitive. She began circling one finger slowly around the swollen button of flesh, feeling it grow even harder at her touch. Unbidden, her morning showers with Tony rose in her mind, his tongue would work her clit, making her insides turn to jelly.

Shaking her head to get Tony out of her mind, she focused on the feel of her fingers on her own clit. She felt a deep thrumming start low in her stomach. Leaning her head against the tile wall, she spread her legs, rubbing her clit with two fingers.

While she was enjoying the familiar sensations of fondling her clit, she slid two fingers of her other hand inside her pussy. She moved her fingers inside herself, trying various speeds and depths. Nothing felt quite the same. Maybe her fingers weren't long enough. It was arousing to finger her pussy, she really didn't do that very often and she wasn't getting the same reaction.

The water from the shower was getting in her mouth so she shifted slightly out of the direct spray. As she moved, her fingers hit that magic spot her husband would normally find. She felt a jolt deep in her stomach and involuntarily bent forward. Oh, this is it, she thought. I've found the magic button.

Excited by this, she probed a bit deeper and found the spot again. She grunted as her body convulsed forward; she couldn't tell by the water of the shower if she was squirting liquid like she did before, but the sensation was very much the same.

Mary experimented with this newfound feeling, finally finding the right depth and position for her fingers. It was awkward standing so she tried kneeling in the shower. The tile was hard, so she grabbed one of the thick hotel towels from the rack and dragged it into the shower with her.

Kneeling on that was much more comfortable. She settled herself on her knees, with the water at her back. It took a moment of probing to find the spot again, when she did it almost doubled her over. She leaned forward, one hand on the shower floor; that was much better.

She now found the spot quickly and she began fingering herself with abandon, curling her fingers as her husband would have done, stroking that sweet spot that sent jolts of orgasmic-like pleasure through her. She looked down at one point, watching between her legs, and saw a squirt of liquid stream out of her pussy.

She wondered how long she could handle this new sensation. It was much easier to control the intensity by fingering herself, but the sensations were quite intense.

Her thumb accidentally brushed her clit at one point; the combined sensation of her probing fingers in her pussy and against her clit was beyond description. Mary adjusted herself again on the towel so she could simultaneously thrust the fingers of one hand inside herself while rubbing her clit with the other. Oh, she thought, this is pure heaven.

Mary lost all track of time, kneeling in the shower. She settled into a pattern; fingering that special spot until she was convulsing repeatedly, and then gently rubbing her clit until that sensation build to a crescendo.

Finally ready for the release of her orgasm, Mary rolled on her back on the towel. She was adept at fingering her clit to reach orgasm and that's what she did, letting the warm water hit her between her legs as she rubbed her clit, working it in circles with her fingers. She began lifting her hips in time with her fingering, the towel giving her feet purchase.

When her orgasm finally broke, it took her completely out of reality. She marched up on the towel, her feet planted, her hips raised in the air as her fingers continued rubbing her clit, giving her an orgasm that seemed endless.

She felt a gush of fluid this time, felt the hot liquid running out of her. She twisted on the towel, her body shaking and quivering. Mary had a split second of panic, that she'd slip or twist and actually hurt herself, but then all thoughts were lost and she gave herself completely over to this incredible orgasm she had given herself.

When she finally came back to reality, her orgasm finally fading, she was lying on her side on the towel, the water still gently caressing her body. She felt weightless, utterly relaxed, and completely sated. She rose slowly from the floor, picking up the sodden towel; in a giddy moment of silliness, she kissed the towel. Thank you, towel, she thought, for being there when I needed you. She held the towel under the water, rinsing away any remnants of her orgasm.

She quickly washed her hair, soaped her body, and rinsed off under the water. She giggled quietly to herself as she wrapped a towel around her body and hair.

It was well past midnight, and it was now Christmas day. She wandered out into the living room and then onto the private terrace of her villa. The moon was still in the sky, although much lower than it had been. "Merry Christmas to you Mary," she muttered to herself, looking up into the sky. A smile finally touched her lips she knew she wasn't alone – her late husband was looking down on her.

CHAPTER 4

ONE NIGHT - AN EROTIC ENCOUNTER

DEAR DIARY,

Today was yet another amazing day at the gym. Although I'd originally gone there for a workout, Michael Harris had taken up most of my time. Why am I so attracted to him? Every time he walks by my heart literally thuds out of my chest. And when he acknowledged my presence today, it almost felt surreal. I know that he has a girlfriend, but from what I hear from the other girls at the gym, their relationship seems to be on the rocks. Either way, he'd be a catch to any woman who had him. The thought of seeing him tomorrow makes my heart melt. I can hardly wait.

Amy closed her diary and tossed it into her drawer. She could hardly believe how much she seemed to be crushing over the hot, young, personal trainer at the gym where she worked out.

Of course, he was a bit younger than she was, but she didn't at all mind. Here she was in her late thirties and still writing stuff into her diary like a silly teenager. Would she ever grow up and get a life? She laughed to herself. Amy

Cranston had been so busy with her career than her love life had taken a back seat.

"There's a difference between career-driven, and crazy workaholic," her friend Lindsey had teased.

Although she hated to admit it, her friend Lindsey was right; she'd become so consumed with her career that she was now a workaholic. It had been over two years since she last went on a date.

But who cares right? It was all about being a strong black woman with her. And so she didn't have the time or the energy to put up with the men around her. Most of them were lying, cheating bastards anyways.

In that moment the image of Michael's lean athletic body, glistening with sweat as he assisted her with her work-out, resurfaced in her mind. She wondered about him, he seemed like one of the few good men around. Flicking through the cards in her wallet, she found the business card she'd been looking for. That of Michael Harris. His telephone number was on it, and she quickly dialed the numbers on her cell phone, waiting anxiously to hear him answer.

"Hello this is Michael," a deep husky voice from the other end of the line sounded through the phone. A part of her wanted to hang up and not pursue whatever was happening between the two of them any further but a part of her the more dominant part wanted Michael, and so she didn't hang up.

"Hi, I was just calling about the dinner date," she felt a little embarrassed at what she was doing. Michael had invited her to dinner weeks ago, and she'd said she would think about it, but never replied until now. Today when she'd seen him at the gym, she was in a way reminded of what she was seemingly missing out on. And so the first thing she'd done when she got home was to write in her diary and then call Michael.

Surprisingly he didn't sound upset or startled to hear her voice. He had pleasantness in his voice that made it all seem all right. And so she inquired where he wanted to go for dinner, what day, and what time.

"How about now, I'm starving," he chuckled.

His statement caught her off guard but she thought about it briefly and happily accepted.

Besides, it would only take her a few minutes to get ready. As they ended their call, Amy hurried off to take a quick shower.

Dinner was beautiful and as they made their way back home, Michael pulled up on the side of the road, into a lonely car park. He dropped the top down on his convertible and cocked his head up to the sky.

Tonight was a beautiful night. Maybe it was the red wine in her system, or the fact that it had been a while since she'd been along with a handsome young man, Amy didn't know, but she could no longer fight the urge to kiss him.

As she captured his lips with hers, he kissed her back with just as much passion. His tongue explored the insides of her mouth feverishly, as his fingers stroked her body. Their kissing intensified and Amy struggled out of her clothes with his help. Once out of the tight red dress that she had owned, her body laid bare before him, the only article of clothing she had left was the thin lace thong.

Michael yanked at the thong until the ripped it off her, and immediately his fingers found her core.

"Oh God, Michael," she moaned her voice laced with passion and desire. Michael's fingers felt amazing as he stroked her moist tender flesh, working his long fingers from her warm slit to her swollen bud. He pinched it lightly, before beginning to massage it between his thumb and index finger.

Amy bit her lips, spreading her legs further and allowing him better access into her temple of delight.

"Good girl, that's what I like," he slipped two fingers into her core and began thrusting inside her. Amy let out several loud ecstatic cries as he pleasured her with his fingers.

Finally, Michael ended his little torture and whipped out his cock. He stroked his erection a few times getting it to the degree of hardness that he wanted.

"I hate this little ole car," he muttered, before inviting her to join him outside in the front of the car.

There was no hesitation on her part, she quickly jumped out of the car, and walked to the front to meet him. He placed both her hands onto the hood of the car, before bending her over with her ass popped out towards him.

Slowly Michael stroked her inner thighs, causing tiny spasms to come crashing down to her temple of delight. A loud moan escaped her lips as he penetrated her core with his massive erection. He pulled out slowly; his cock glistened from her wetness. Without warning, he gave her a hard powerful thrust, burying his shaft inside her.

Amy's body yelped as he continued to serve her with a series of long hard thrusts mixed with shorter quicker thrusts. Each time she would beg him for more. As he continued to move in and out of her wetness, Amy found herself getting closer and closer to her amazing climax. Closing her eyes, she parted her legs further as he penetrated her temple of delight relentlessly.

Waves of pleasure coursed through her body. Michael rammed his cock deep down into her.

He let out several loud ecstatic groans with each hard thrust. As she summited her climax, Amy cried out in delirium. Soon after her orgasm, Michael found himself approaching his climax. With a loud thunderous groan and hard thrust, he exploded his load of semen into her pussy.

Their juices combined and slowly slipped out of her. It took them a minute to calm down from their brief moment of pleasure.

As they drove home, Amy could hardly wait to log her erotic experience with Michael in her good ole journal.

CHAPTER 5

SONG OF PASSION

"SOUNDED GREAT, Hannah. I think we got it," Brody Conner said into Hannah's ear through her headphones in the recording booth.

She smiled back at him and took the headphones off. She left the booth and entered the production room. Brody's green eyes smiled down at her. His sandy blonde hair was rumpled as usual.

"You're on fire today, girl," he told her and patted her shoulder.

Hannah said, "Thanks. I'm glad we were able to get it done. Will has been on our ass all week about it."

Brody nodded. "Yeah, I know. Now we can just do the mixing and we'll be finished."

Hannah took a sip of her water and then said, "Thanks for all your help," and laid her hand on his arm.

The contact seemed to burn through Brody and he looked down at Hannah's pretty hand. He'd wanted her for so long. He wondered what Hannah would do if he told her. Brody decided that it was time to find out. He took her hand and kissed the back of it. Then he looked into her warm brown eyes and smiled at the surprise he saw there.

"You're so beautiful," he said. His gaze dipped to her full mouth and the urge to kiss her was strong. "I've wanted to tell you how much I like you for a while now."

Hannah couldn't believe what she was hearing. She'd had a crush on Brody since she'd first saw him four months ago. She'd figured that he hadn't noticed her even though she wore enticing outfits and talked to him a lot.

"Really?" she asked. "I had no idea. I like you, too, in that way."

Now it was Brody's turn to be surprised. "Wow. I had no idea, either." Hannah shook her head. "Both of us kept quiet all this time."

Brody's eyes took on an unfamiliar light as he looked at Hannah. "I'm not keeping quiet anymore," he said and closed the distance between them.

Hannah's breath caught in her throat as she felt the heat from his body invade her personal space. His T-shirt showed off his finely sculpted chest and his jeans were tight enough that they outlined his package. Hannah began to see him naked in her mind's eye and she wanted to make that happen for real.

She looked up at him and saw the same thoughts mirrored in his eyes. Brody dipped his head and caught her mouth in a deep, blistering kiss. Their tongues met, teased, and twined with each other. When they broke apart, both of them were a little breathless.

"Damn," Brody said. He let his gaze travel over her hot, Latina body. He wanted to see all of her luscious, curvy body. Without a word, Brody stepped to the door of the production room and closed and locked it. He closed the observation curtains. They were completely alone and had plenty of privacy.

Brody took off his T-shirt and Hannah's eyes roved hungrily over his bare chest and powerful arms. The man might not give much attention to his hair, but he obviously worked hard on the rest of his body.

She took off her own shirt, revealing a black satiny bra. Her breasts created crescent moons above the bra and Brody wanted to kiss them. He unbuttoned his cargo pants and pulled the zipper down. In response, Hannah unzipped her skirt and let it almost fall. They seemed to have entered a "you show me yours and I'll show you mine" phase.

Brody pushed his pants all the way down to his ankles giving Hannah a perfect view of his nether regions. He was certainly well endowed. Hannah's skirt and underwear followed suit along with her bra.

They came together quickly, each wanting to touch and taste each other everywhere. Brody bent and sucked her nipples, biting and licking the turgid peaks. Hannah moaned and ran her hands through his wavy hair. She felt the pulling pressure Brody created and the sensations ran through her body and made her pussy tingle.

Brody ran his hand down her smooth-skinned side and then brought it around to cup her shaved mound. He stroked her pussy lips lightly and Hannah shivered at the contact. She felt so good against his palm. He moved from her tits to kneeling on the floor and delving his tongue between her pussy lips.

Hannah gasped when he found her clit and licked it with his smooth, wet tongue. She was so excited and wanted more of what he was doing.

"That feels incredible," she said.

Brody replied, "You taste incredible. Come here."

She didn't quite know what to think when he laid down on the floor of the production booth.

Brody saw her confusion and said, "Sit on my face. Straddle it."

Hannah knelt on the floor by his head and then swung her leg over his head. "Is that right?" She'd never done anything like that before.

Brody nodded. "Mmmhmm." He spread her pussy open and went back to licking her clit.

Hannah sighed and let her head fall back as Brody set about pleasuring her. A sweet pressure built inside her and thrummed all along her nerves. Brody licked and sucked Hannah's clit enjoying her taste while he nudged her further towards bliss. Hannah started moving her hips and Brody held her still. She gave a little whimper as her climax began, trying to keep quiet since someone could be passing by in the hall outside.

It flowed through Hannah keeping her motionless as pleasure gripped her. She made breathy little moans that told Brody that she was cumming. After a few moments, he let up and smiled at Hannah.

"Did you like that?"

She laughed. "You know I did smartass."

Brody slid out from between her legs. "Yeah, I could tell."

"Come here," Hannah said as she caught sight of his big dick. It was half-erect and she wanted to make it stand up completely.

Brody took a couple of steps until he was right in front of her and watched her take his cock in her hands and stroke it. When her warm mouth closed over the head, Brody groaned and stroked Hannah's sleek black hair. Hannah went to work on Brody's cock in earnest. She licked around the head, not missing the small hole in the center. She tickled around the head and took Brody's shaft deep into her mouth. She worked in and out, sucking as she went. Brody knew he couldn't take much more; it felt too good.

He said, "Hannah, that feels so good, but I want to be inside you."

Hannah pulled back and smiled at him. "I want you inside me with that big

dick."

She lay back on the floor and put her legs up in the air. Then Hannah shook

her ass, enticing Brody further. He knelt and guided his cock into her sweet, pink cunt. She was tight and wet and Brody thought he'd never felt anything so good before. He began moving, thrusting and pulling back in an increasingly fast rhythm.

Hannah wrapped her legs around Brody's waist and grabbed his back, giving herself up to his passionate tempo. Blissful sensations ran through her and she let out small moans of delight. Brody made his own noises of passion as they thrust against each other.

Hannah gave a short cry and then bit Brody's shoulder as she came. Brody felt the pulses of her pussy around his dick and then felt his own orgasm begin. It was a powerful thing and Brody gave a low growl and thrust forward one last time as their mutual climax kept them willing prisoners for long moments.

Slowly Brody let himself down on top of Hannah and he kissed her gently. He looked into her beautiful dark eyes. "I know that this wasn't exactly romantic, but-"

"Are you kidding? It was hot!" Hannah protested. She

loved that their first time together was in the recording studio where they made so much music together. She kissed him and whispered that she was happy that they were now making a different kind of music together.

Brody smiled at her and said, "We're making our very own love song." "That's right, and we're gonna keep on making it for a long, long time,"

Hannah agreed and soon they were lost in each other all over again.

ABOUT THE AUTHOR

Fae DeRose is an emerging erotica author of many erotica kinks and sub-genres. Be sure to check out other books and leave a review if this story got you hot!

Visit my blog at Fae DeRose Blog

Join my newsletter for the exclusive Fae DeRose Newsletter

Sign up for Free Stories from Xplicit Press Authors

Xplicit Press Author Updates

Like Xplicit Press on Facebook

Follow Xplicit Press on Twitter

Readers: I want to expand a few of the stories to see where the characters can be explored further. If there are any of the stories that you would like to read more about again, I'd love to hear from you!

Keep In Touch
Fae DeRose
info@faederose.com

www.ingramcontent.com/pod-product-compliance
Lightning Source LLC
Chambersburg PA
CBHW020824150626
46554CB00018B/2453